HORSELAND

# Trail Ride Terror

Adapted by
**ANNIE AUERBACH**

Based on the episode
**"FIRE, FIRE,
BURNING BRIGHT"**

Written by
**ERIC LEWALD**
and **JULIA LEWALD**

HarperEntertainment
*An Imprint of HarperCollinsPublishers*

Horseland #3: Trail Ride Terror
Copyright © 2007 DIC Entertainment Corp.
Horseland property™ Horseland LCC
Printed in the United States of America.

For information address HarperCollins Children's Books, a division of HarperCollins Publishers,
1350 Avenue of the Americas, New York, NY 10019.
www.harpercollinschildrens.com
www.horseland.com

Library of Congress catalog card number: 2007926272
ISBN 978-0-06-134169-4

Book design by Sean Boggs
❖
First Edition

# CHAPTER 1

**H**orseland is a wonderful sprawling ranch located in the middle of beautiful countryside. With a large stable, a tackroom, and best of all, an arena for training, Horseland is the greatest place around to board, groom, and show a horse. It's also the ideal spot for making lasting friendships. But high above the expansive ranch of Horseland, a section of the nearby forest shows signs of terrible destruction.

Charred branches litter the ground near the small lake, and the smell of smoke still hangs in the air—reminders of recent events. Three of Horseland's animal residents, Shep, Teeny, and Angora, walk through the area, surveying the damage.

"Eww! What a mess!" exclaims Teeny.

The potbellied pig doesn't like anything messy or dirty.

Shep wrinkles his nose at the burnt smell in the air. "Who knew humans could do so much damage in one night?" he asks. The Australian shepherd herding dog often gives humans the benefit of the doubt, but seeing the destruction firsthand is shocking.

"Yeah, but they're *our* humans, remember?" Teeny points out. "Give them a break. Accidents happen."

"Hmph!" says Angora the cat. "Ever notice that when *responsible* humans are careful, there aren't nearly so many accidents?"

Shep gives her a puzzled look. "How would you know anything about responsibility?" he asks. "All you're responsible for is sleeping, eating, and grooming."

"Stop it!" Teeny says suddenly, fed up with Shep and Angora constantly arguing. "The most important thing is that our humans got home safe," she reminded them. "Don't you see that?"

Shep and Angora exchange looks. Teeny isn't often the logical one among them.

"I guess so," Shep admits.

"For once, I agree," says Angora.

Teeny smiles. "Thank you," she says, happy she made her point.

"Shep," says Angora, turning to the dog. "You're just lucky you didn't go along like you wanted to."

"I wish I had. Then I could have helped," Shep replies with a heavy sigh. "I remember the morning they left. . . ."

# CHAPTER 2

**O**ne pretty summer morning, a lot of activity was going on at Horseland Ranch. Sarah Whitney, Will Taggert, Molly Washington, Alma Rodriguez, and sisters Chloe and Zoey Stilton were busy packing saddlebags and prepping their horses for an overnight camping trip. Just outside the gate, Shep watched the group make their final preparations for the journey.

5

"I don't understand why I can't go on this trip," complained Shep. "They need me. How can I look after the horses when they're miles away?"

It was Shep's responsibility at Horseland to keep the horses in line. Not being able to join them on this trip felt very frustrating for him.

Behind Shep, Angora was trying to keep her balance on a set of hay bales that wobbled as Teeny used them to scratch her back.

"The kids are old enough to take good care of the horses by now," Teeny reassured the dog. "Besides, that campsite is a long waddle away. Not a bucket of slop to be found for miles!" Teeny had a healthy appetite and was happy to be staying at Horseland—where the food was!

Angora stretched luxuriously on the top hay bale and then settled down in preparation for a little nap. "I hope they get lost for a while," she said. "Maybe then we'll have a little peace and quiet around here."

Shep disagreed. "I like it better when everyone's together."

At fourteen years old, Will was the most experienced rider of the group. He was also the nephew of Mr. and Mrs. Handler, who owned Horseland. Will and his palomino stallion, Jimber, would be leading everyone on the trail ride. Once they reached the campsite, he would also be in charge.

Will walked around the riders as they loaded up their gear. "Everyone packed up and ready to go?" he asked the group.

"Sure am!" Sarah replied.

"Yup!" Chloe called out.

"You betcha!" Molly said enthusiastically.

Will wanted to make sure everyone had packed properly. First, he inspected Alma's gear, which was already secured onto Button, her skewbald pinto mare. Alma lovingly petted Button's beautiful white mane.

"Nice work, Alma," Will told her, testing the straps with a yank. "That'll hold just fine."

"Thanks, Will," replied Alma happily. Alma's father was the stable manager at Horseland, so she'd had plenty of experience around horses.

Next, Will approached Molly and the heap of stuff perched atop Calypso, her spotted Appaloosa mare. A suitcase, a pillow, and even a teddy bear! At the first sign of a full gallop, everything was bound to fall off.

Will shook his head and smiled. "Ten points for style, Molly, but I'm not sure that's going to make it past the gate," he told her.

"Oh, Will, you're no fun!" teased Molly, as she began to untie the towering gear. You could always count on Molly's good attitude.

Will continued down the line, where

Chloe and Zoey were waiting for his inspection. "And what have we here?" he asked, walking up to their horses, Chili and Pepper, both gray Dutch Warmbloods.

"Two days of supplies," replied Chloe. "Just like you said."

"We are *so* prepared," Zoey added confidently.

"You look a little *over*prepared to me," said Will, looking at the bulging bags. He unstrapped a saddlebag and reached inside. He pulled out a hair dryer and held it up. "You must be kidding," he said, cocking his head to one side.

The sisters just looked at him innocently. They were spoiled and rich, and they were used to having the best and most luxurious things around them.

"Where are you planning to plug this in?" Will asked with a chuckle, as he held up the hair dryer.

Chloe and Zoey traded looks. *No hair dryer?*

"A girl *has* to look her best," Chloe said with a flick of her long strawberry blond hair.

Zoey nodded in agreement.

"Can't you bring an extension cord?" Chloe asked Will in a hopeful voice.

Will shot Chloe a disbelieving look and then removed one of Pepper's saddlebags.

"Let's reorganize some of this," he said, just as some of the contents spilled out. "Whoa!"

Out of the saddlebag tumbled an MP3 player, sunglasses, a mirror, a brush, a pair of keys, and a makeup bag.

"Hey! We need that stuff!" insisted Zoey.

"Sorry, but what about packing some *camping* supplies instead?" suggested Will. He pointed to a stack of pots and pans and other equipment nearby.

"What?!" cried Zoey. "How many pots do we really need?" She couldn't believe a pot was more important than her lip gloss.

Will took a deep breath. "Chloe, Zoey, everybody has responsibilities on the trip that affect the whole group. If there's trouble, we've got to be ready to handle anything." He bent down, picked up a first-aid kit, and opened it up. "For instance, a first-aid kit is an absolute must—especially when there's a cell phone inside. It's programmed to call Horseland's emergency numbers." He handed the cell phone and kit to the girls and left them to do some serious repacking.

Zoey looked at the cell phone. "Preprogrammed numbers? What fun is that?" she said. She handed the phone to her sister to put away.

"Yeah. Besides, what trouble could we get into on a little camping trip?" wondered Chloe.

Zoey looked over at the rest of the group and shook her head. "I don't get it. Everyone else is so seriously prepared. Why do *we* have to bring anything?" As usual, Zoey was thinking only about herself.

Grudgingly, the sisters picked up the supplies from the pile and brought them over to their horses. Then they began to repack the saddlebags.

Meanwhile, one rider wasn't going on the trip: Bailey Handler. The son of Horseland's owners, Bailey was busy inside the stable, tossing hay into the stalls with a pitchfork as the others prepared for their trip. He was frustrated and disappointed at having to stay behind. His horse, Aztec, a Kiger mustang, watched from his stall. The horse wished that they were going, too.

"'*Somebody* has to stay and get the chores done, Bailey,'" the boy said, repeating what he was told. "'There will be *other* camping trips, Bailey.'"

Aztec whinnied, and Bailey looked up. He chuckled. "Oh, well, Aztec. Maybe it'll rain on them!" he said with a wink.

# CHAPTER 3

It was a beautiful day for a trail ride. The sun shone down brightly, and the air was clean and warm. The six horses and their riders climbed their way up through a wooded area of the mountains, riding two by two through the tall trees.

"We're coming to a meadow," Will announced from the front of the line. "We can give the horses some rein."

"Thank goodness," said Chloe. She was bored with the trail already.

Before long, a large, grassy meadow came into view. A few orange butterflies flew overhead, and a bird soared on the gentle breeze that swept across the meadow. The six horses eagerly galloped through the field, interrupting the calmness. The riders pulled on their horses' reins, and they all came to a stop to take a look around. Scenic

mountain peaks and lush woodlands surrounded them.

Sarah pushed her long hair behind her ears and looked around as she sat astride Scarlet, her black Arabian mare. "Oh, Will! This is beautiful!" she exclaimed.

Will grinned. "Sure is," he replied. "Worth the whole ride just to see this."

However, two girls didn't see what the big deal was.

"Uh . . . how much longer until the campsite?" asked Chloe impatiently. The trail ride had been much longer than she had anticipated.

Her freckle-faced sister was just as impatient. She couldn't understand why the campsite was so far away. "You'd think one patch of dirt would be as good as another," Zoey grumbled.

Just then, Molly urged Calypso forward into a gallop. Her horse's mane blew back in the breeze. "Last one across the meadow does the dishes!" Molly called out to the others, as she raced away.

The rest of the group sprang into action and hurried to catch up.

"Giddyup, Button!" Alma said to her horse.

"Go, boy!" Chloe urged Chili.

At the back, Will raised his hand to object. "Now hold on a sec—" But all the girls were already on their way. Will laughed and patted Jimber. "Aw, why not? Come on, Jimber. Let's show them how it's done!"

Jimber neighed and shook his black-and-golden mane. Then he reared up and took off, thundering across the grass.

The horses joyfully galloped across the gorgeous meadow, each rider intent on being the first one to the campsite. Molly was in the lead, with Alma and Sarah close behind her. Farther back, Chloe and Zoey were surprised to see Will overtake them.

"Galloping feels good, doesn't it?" Alma said to Sarah, as they rode side by side.

"Yeah," answered Sarah. "Especially when I'm . . . in the lead!" With that, she rode Scarlet even harder and pulled ahead of Alma. She and Scarlet made a great team, and before long, they had even passed Molly and Calypso.

"Wow!" cried Molly. "Look at Sarah go!" Then Molly turned her head and was in for a surprise: Everyone else was passing her by!

"Hey! Now I'm totally last!" she shouted.

Meanwhile, Will and Jimber were gaining ground. Jimber was a strong horse, and he put all he had into catching up to Scarlet.

Sarah looked over her shoulder. "Will's trying to catch us, Scarlet," she said to her horse. "Come on, girl. Let's lose him!" They charged forward.

In a last attempt, Jimber surged forward, but he just couldn't catch up to Scarlet. Sarah and Scarlet reached the campsite first. Sarah reined in her horse and slowly came to a stop.

"Oh yeah!" cheered Sarah. She happily punched her fist in the air. "Good run, Scarlet!" she said, as she caressed her horse's neck.

Scarlet snorted and whinnied proudly.

"Good one, Sarah," said Will, as he reached the other end of the meadow and slowed Jimber.

Just then, the rest of the group rode up—with Molly arriving last.

Molly shook her head and sighed. "Oh, why did I call, 'Last one in washes dishes'?" she wondered aloud.

Chloe and Zoey were quick to make excuses why they didn't come in first. They both hated losing, even if it was just supposed to be a fun game.

"That wasn't a *real* test of horses *or* riding," Chloe declared.

"I know," agreed her sister. "It only matters when there's a panel of judges." Zoey bent over and patted Pepper's neck. "Pepper always rides better with an audience."

Will had heard enough and decided that it was time to get moving again. "The camp-site is just over that ridge," he announced, changing the subject.

Sarah smiled. "Let's get that campfire started and break out the marshmallows!"

# CHAPTER 4

Over the ridge, the horses and their riders came into a clearing. They stopped near the center, where there was a group of stones arranged in a circle, just perfect for a campfire. Will dismounted Jimber and started assigning chores.

"Take your bags and saddles off your horses and rub them down," he instructed. "Alma, start getting the tents set up."

"Aye, aye, Captain Will," Alma said with a salute. She got down off of Button and immediately got to work.

"Molly, you unpack the food and utensils," Will said. "And remember to boil all the water we use for cooking or drinking."

"Got it, Will," replied Molly, throwing a saddlebag over her shoulder.

Sarah was next. "Sarah, there are some dead branches back toward the meadow," Will told her.

"*Saw* them," replied Sarah with a giggle. She held out a small, folding wood saw. "Get it?"

"Very funny," Will answered with a smile. "Glad you're on it."

Zoey and Chloe dismounted from their horses and brushed themselves off.

"After this campout, we should get some serious spa treatments," Zoey said to her sister.

Chloe couldn't agree more. She started thinking about all the treatments she would

indulge in: massage, facial, manicure, pedi-cure . . .

However, Will had plenty for the sisters to do before then. He tossed them four col-lapsible plastic jugs.

"There's a lake just over the hill," Will

explained. "We'll need all four water jugs filled."

Chloe put her hands on her hips. "I thought we came here to get *away* from chores!" she moaned.

"Yeah," Zoey said snottily. She looked directly at Will. "Some vacation!"

Will simply shrugged. "Fine. No water means no supper. So which one of you wants to tell the others?"

Chloe and Zoey looked at each other and then at the empty water jugs.

"All right, all right," Chloe said finally. "Looks like we're water maidens."

Will nodded approvingly. "When you go camping, you depend on each other. Everybody does his or her share," he told the girls. Then he turned on his heel and left them to their duty.

The girls picked up the jugs and headed off toward the lake.

"I'd say carrying all four of these things full of water is *way* more than our share,"

complained Chloe.

"Right," agreed Zoey. "No way I'm lugging that much water up a hill!" Then she tossed one of her two water jugs right into the bushes! "Much better now."

Chloe was surprised—but intrigued. "Let me give it a try." She pitched the empty jug over her head and into the bushes. She grinned. "You're right, Zoey, this is *much* better."

Then the girls continued on their way to the lake, each holding one empty water jug.

Once the humans were out of sight, busily taking care of setting up camp, the horses began to talk among themselves.

"Listen to those humans complain," said Jimber. He was appalled. "You'd think we'd ridden on *their* backs up that mountain!"

"C'mon, Jimber. They're just kids," Calypso said, trying to lighten the mood.

"I'll bet you pitched a shoe or two when you were a colt."

"I don't think Jimber was ever a colt," Button said playfully. "He was born old." She and Button laughed.

Jimber just sighed. It was going to be a long night.

# CHAPTER
## 5

That evening, with the moon and stars overhead, Will, Alma, Sarah, Chloe, and Zoey sat around a glowing campfire. Each of the girls held a long stick with a few marshmallows at the end of it over the crackling fire. But their focus was on Will, who was in the middle of telling a scary story.

"... and then they hear the scratching again, right outside the passenger-side door," said Will. "Becky Sue slams the lock down on the door and screams, 'Go! Go! Go!'"

The girls listened with increasing anticipation, their eyes growing wider by the second. Sarah and Alma were practically holding their breath.

Will continued, his voice growing louder and more intense. "When Billy turns the key, the engine tries and tries, but it won't start! The scratching gets louder . . . then the door handle starts clicking! But the car *still* won't start. And then . . . with a big *thump*, something lands on the roof!"

*BANG! CLANG!*

The girls gasped in fright.

But it was only Molly. She had been listening to the scary story, too. She had dropped the pots and pans she had been cleaning—her punishment for coming in last in the race earlier.

"Oops, sorry," she said sheepishly.

The other girls sighed in relief. Then they urged Will to finish his story.

"Then the car starts, and they speed away, tearing through the night until they get back to Becky Sue's house," Will said. "They're home. They're safe. But as Becky Sue opens the car door, she hears a skittering, like claws on metal. And then the ravenous animals are upon her! Becky Sue screams! *Aaaaahhh!!!*"

"*Aaaahhhh!!!*" screamed the five girls in response.

Then Will smiled and said calmly, "Then the pair of squirrels grab her bag of popcorn and run off into the night."

All the girls laughed. Will certainly knew the right way to tell a scary campfire story!

"Great, now how are we are going to get to sleep?" asked Sarah.

"Tell us another one!" Molly said to Will.

"Nah," replied Will, standing up. "That's the classic. The others aren't as good. Anyway, it's time to shut down for the night."

Alma got to her feet and stretched. Then she went to see Button, who was tethered nearby with the other horses. "Good night, girl," she said, patting Button's nose. "I'll be right over there in my tent."

Meanwhile, Will had picked up two of the water jugs. One was already empty, and the other wasn't even half full. He walked back to the campfire, where Chloe and Zoey were still sitting, and pointed to the water jug.

"There's not much left here to douse the fire, but the other two jugs you filled should be plenty," Will said to the sisters.

Chloe and Zoey exchanged a quick glance.

"Uh . . . other two jugs . . . right," said Chloe, trying to sound as if nothing were wrong.

"Yeah . . . the other two jugs," said Zoey, nodding.

Will left the one jug and headed to his tent. When he was out of sight, Zoey turned to her sister.

"I told you we should have filled all the jugs," Zoey whispered.

"No, you didn't!" Chloe whispered back, her hands on her hips.

"So what are we going to do?" worried Zoey.

"Well, I'm not going back down to the lake in the dark!" Chloe insisted, as she stood up. She picked up the jug with the remaining water in it and dumped it on the fire. The flame went out, and only a few embers were still burning. Chloe kicked some dirt on them.

"That's good enough, right?" asked Zoey.

"Who's going to know?" answered

Chloe with a sneaky smile. "By the time we get up, the fire will have been out for hours."

The sisters snuggled down into their sleeping bags, unaware that their secret wouldn't stay safe for long.

# CHAPTER 6

Later that night, all of the kids were sleeping peacefully in their tents. They had no idea what was happening only a few feet away. . . .

A little breeze had picked up, blowing through some branches in the trees. The breeze continued on, reaching the remaining campfire embers, which began to smolder and spark. The sparks made contact with some leftover dry kindling—and a fire began!

The horses shifted anxiously and yanked at their tethered harnesses as smoke quickly filled the air.

Smoke drifted into Will's tent, and he woke up with a start. He heard the horses whinnying outside. "Jimber!" he called out. Then he sniffed the air and a look of panic crossed his face. "FIRE!"

Will leaped out of his tent and shouted, "Everybody get up!" He looked around and saw the nearby trees ablaze. The fire was spreading fast!

Sarah was the next one awake. "Will, what is it?" she asked, coming out of her tent. She was shocked by the flames all around them.

"Help me untie the horses!" shouted Will.

Alarmed, the horses frantically reared and tugged at their harnesses. Will and Sarah immediately set about untying all of them.

"What happened?" Sarah shouted over the crackling sounds of the fire.

"I don't know," replied Will. "But we've got to get everybody over toward the lake."

"Fire!" Will shouted again. "Everybody up!"

At that moment, Molly and Alma peeked out of their tent and screamed. They scrambled out into the intense heat and headed straight to their horses.

Chloe and Zoey groggily came out of their tent. They weren't sure what was going

on. Suddenly they looked up and saw a burning tree branch about to fall on them!

*"Aaaahhh!!!"* they screamed.

"Uh-oh!" exclaimed Will. He raced over to the girls and moved them away from the tent. "Come on!"

The three of them fled just in time. The flaming branch came down with a *thud*— right on Zoey and Chloe's tent. It set the tent ablaze within seconds.

"Run!" Will ordered, and the girls ran off toward the lake. Then he turned back toward the fire. "I've got to go back and get something."

Meanwhile, the horses were racing toward the lake, hoping to find safety. Suddenly, Jimber slowed and asked the others to do the same. He reminded them that their humans were still behind them.

Sure enough, the five girls were running through the smoky woods, breathing hard. Still dressed in their pajamas, they had time to grab only their riding helmets.

Sarah glanced over her shoulder. Suddenly, she came to an abrupt stop.

"Hey! Stop!" she called to the others. "Where's Will?"

The other girls looked around. They thought Will was with them. Where had he gone?

# CHAPTER 7

"Will!"

"Will!!"

Worried for their friend, the girls nervously called out and frantically looked around.

At that moment, Will stumbled toward them from the wall of smoke, eyes watering and coughing.

"Thank goodness!" Sarah cried with relief when she saw him.

49

That's when Alma noticed that Will was carrying something. "Why did you go back to get your stuff?" she said to him. "You could have been hurt!"

"I stayed well away from the fire. But I had to go," explained Will. "I knew we'd need *this*." He opened the first-aid kit he was holding and took out the cell phone. He deliberately looked at Chloe and Zoey and said, "Glad we didn't leave it behind at Horseland."

Zoey got his meaning but didn't take the bait. Instead, she smiled and said, "Yeah. Good thing Chloe and I packed it!"

Will gave them a quick smirk. Then he suggested they all head away from the fire immediately. There was no time to lose!

While the group was escaping the blazing fire in the woods, Bailey was safely at home in bed, snoring and dreaming away.

*BRRRING!!!*

The ringing phone jolted him out of his slumber, and tangled in sheets and blankets, Bailey fell right off the bed and hit the floor with a *thump!*

"Huh? Hey, what's that?" Bailey said groggily, as the phone continued to ring. Finally, he realized what was going on and turned on the light. Bleary-eyed, he picked up the phone.

"This better be good," he muttered into the phone. "Do you have a clue what time it is?"

Suddenly, his eyes widened with surprise. He was instantly awake, alert, and listening closely.

"Yeah, Will. Got it. I'll get the word out," Bailey told him. "Just keep everybody safe."

# CHAPTER
## 8

**T**he six horses and their riders made it safely to the edge of the moonlit lake. Behind them, the woods appeared to be glowing, as smoke and flames rose above the tree line.

Sarah grabbed hold of Scarlet's halter in one hand and gently petted her with the other. "It's going to be okay, girl," she murmured to her horse. "We're all here now."

"Now what?" asked Alma. "That fire's spreading."

Will took charge. "Everyone, get on your horse and follow me," he said.

As everyone put on their riding helmets, Molly asked, "What are we going to do for saddles?"

"We'll ride bareback," said Sarah. "We've all done it around the stables."

Chloe looked at her horse. "How about it, Chili?"

The horse whinnied his approval.

"Let's give it a try, Pepper," said Zoey, as she climbed onto her horse.

Alma walked over to Molly and helped her climb up onto Calypso.

"What about you, Alma?" Molly asked.

Alma smiled. "Button and I have been working on a new trick," she said. Then she whistled, and Button trotted over to her and kneeled down. Alma easily climbed on her back.

"Nice one!" said Molly, giving her a thumbs-up.

Once all the girls were mounted on their horses, Will called out, "Follow me!"

Holding on tight to their horses' reins, they raced down a trail, keeping the lake in view. Will knew it was important to be near the water. The riders slid around a bit on their horses, and some of the girls secretly wished for their saddles.

"Whoa!" cried Chloe.

"So-o-o bump-y!" exclaimed Zoey.

In the lead, Will suddenly pulled up

short. The other riders stopped behind him and looked alarmed as they saw more fire up ahead.

"The fire's cut us off!" announced Will. Now there was no way they could take that route.

Molly rode up to Will. "Now what?" she asked, trying not to sound frightened.

Will turned Jimber around and led the group in the opposite direction. Before long, Will pulled up short again. Another escape route was blocked, as the fire grew larger, consuming everything in its path.

"Oh, no!" cried Sarah.

"The fire is cutting off every trail!" exclaimed Molly.

Realizing that they were trapped, they found it hard to keep calm.

"What are we going to do?" worried Alma.

Sarah watched with horror as the flames spread dangerously close to them. "Into the lake! It's our only chance!" she called.

Molly tried to be upbeat. "Yeah, nothing like swimming in your pajamas!"

As the group once again headed down the steep mountainside toward the lake, Chloe and Zoey hung back, looking anxious.

"Did they say we're going to swim?" said Chloe uneasily.

Zoey bit her lip nervously. "Couldn't we try another way?" she asked.

"We just tried the other ways!" Alma

called out, as she headed down.

Chloe and Zoey were hesitant, but they nervously urged their horses forward, following the others down to the lake.

At the lake, Will was on the ground, pulling Jimber through the shallow water. Once it got deeper, he would hop on Jimber's back.

"Come on!" said Will. "We're running out of time!"

Sarah, Molly, and Alma jumped off their horses and followed Will's lead into the water.

When Chloe and Zoey got there, Chloe shook her head. "No way!" she said. She wouldn't even get off her horse, let alone get in the water. Zoey wouldn't budge either.

From the lake, Sarah turned back to see that the girls weren't moving. "Chloe, Zoey, what's the problem?" asked Sarah.

Chloe and Zoey gulped and blurted out, "We can't swim!"

# CHAPTER 9

**A**lma couldn't believe what she just heard. "You can't swim?" she asked Chloe and Zoey. The sisters were still on shore, astride their horses.

"Don't you guys have an Olympic-sized pool to go with your mansion-sized home?" Molly asked.

Chloe nodded. "Yeah, but chlorine dries your skin out," she explained.

Molly led Calypso out of the water and

back to the shore. "Let me get this straight," said Molly. "You got all the way to middle school without learning to swim?"

Chloe looked away, shamefaced. She knew it was embarrassing. Luckily, at that moment, Sarah approached them.

"No time to discuss this now," Sarah told them. "Not when the fire is getting so close!"

She was right. The fire was getting nearer to the lake's edge, as flames engulfed many of the trees, sending them crashing down.

"One of you can hang onto me," Alma said to Chloe and Zoey. "I'm a strong swimmer."

Chloe and Zoey were surprised by Alma's offer. They knew deep inside that they would never be that selfless in a similar situation.

But Will disagreed with Alma's suggestion. "No way," he said, making his way back to shore. "It's a long way across the lake.

Even a good swimmer could get dragged down by the extra weight."

"Hmph! I don't weigh *that* much!" Chloe said, crossing her arms.

Will furrowed his brow. "Let me think . . ."

Jimber's head snapped to the left as a burning tree branch fell close to the group. He whinnied and spun around, heading back into the water where Button and Scarlet were waiting.

Molly cried out when Calypso also followed Jimber back into the water.

"What is wrong with those humans?" Jimber said angrily. "Don't they know enough to get out of the way of a fire?"

The other horses whinnied and reared, hoping to draw their riders away from the fire.

Will looked at the agitated horses and had
an idea. "Everyone! Get on your horses!"

Sarah, Alma, and Molly splashed through
the water and mounted their horses.
Meanwhile, Will stood in the water and

grabbed Chili and Pepper's reins.

"Come on, you two. Hold on," Will said to Chloe and Zoey, who had never dismounted. "We can do this!" Then he led them into the water.

"Everyone, grab onto their manes and hold on tight!" Will called out to the group.

The group did as Will instructed, and the horses began swimming.

"That's right, we'll be across in no time," Sarah said reassuringly to Scarlet.

"Come on, Chili. Come on, Pepper," Will said, as he eased them farther into the lake. Then he dropped their reins and mounted Jimber, hoping the other two horses would follow him. "Zoey and Chloe, you're going to be okay."

Chloe shook with fear. "I can't do this!" she cried.

Suddenly, a flaming branch fell into the water right next to the girls. They gasped. The raging fire was getting closer by the minute!

"Yes, I *can* do this!" Chloe quickly decided.

With a gentle tug of the reins and a squeal of fear, Chloe and Zoey eased their horses into the water, following the others.

"Will!" Zoey cried out. "What if I fall off?"

"Will!" Chloe whimpered. "I'm scared!"

"Just hold on tight," Will reassured them. "You'll be fine."

Just then Jimber neighed restlessly. He wanted to move forward.

"Easy, boy," Will said to Jimber, patting his horse's neck. "We need to stay near Chloe and Zoey, in case they need us."

Sarah, Alma, and Molly sat astride their horses as the strong, brave animals swam through the water toward the other side of the lake. The girls were up to their waists in chilly water, but putting distance between them and the fire was all that mattered.

"Is everybody okay?" Alma asked.

Molly looked behind her. "Chloe and

Zoey are okay," she said. Then she giggled. "I hear them squealing."

Chloe and Zoey were indeed squealing—mostly out of nervousness. But they were also shivering from being in the cold water.

"Chili, try to go faster," urged Chloe. "You must be freezing, too!"

Slowly and steadily, the entire group made it safely across the lake.

"Finally!" exclaimed Chloe, getting off of Chili. "LAND!"

Everyone was grateful to have reached the other side of the lake. Each of them dismounted and then immediately attended to his or her horse.

Scarlet shivered from the cold. Sarah did her best to soothe her. "Good girl, Scarlet. I didn't know you were such a good swimmer!"

Calypso playfully shook out her mane, the water spraying all over Molly.

"Hey! Watch it, Calypso!" Molly said with a giggle. "I'm wet enough already!"

Alma gave Button a hug. "Thanks for the ride," she said gratefully to her horse. Then she turned to Will. "Now we wait, right?" she asked, as she wrung out the water from her long, brown hair.

"Yup," replied Will. "We're safe here."

# CHAPTER 10

**A**lma, Sarah, and Molly huddled together up against a rock, hugging each other for warmth. Chloe and Zoey sat by themselves against another rock. It was a chilly night, and their wet pajamas weren't helping the situation.

"W-who knew it could feel so c-c-cold in the summer?" Molly said, shivering.

Across the lake, the fire roared on. But up

above, a helicopter was busy at work, drop-
ping water over the wildfire, while firefighters battled the blaze on the ground.

"Who knew I'd be so glad to see firefighters?" said Sarah.

"So who's going to mention which one
of us was in charge of dousing our campfire?" Alma wondered, glancing over at
Chloe and Zoey.

"Actually," began Sarah, "there's someone
else I'm more worried about right now."
She looked over at Will, who was sitting
alone on a tree stump near the lake, his chin
resting on his hands. Sarah walked up to him
and kneeled down.

"You blame yourself for the fire, don't
you?" she asked him.

"Who else?" Will said angrily, looking
the other way.

"We were all given responsibilities," said
Sarah. "It's not your fault that Chloe and
Zoey didn't live up to theirs."

Will shook his head. "But *I* was in charge

of the trip," he insisted. "*I'm* responsible for everyone."

"And you did a great job," Sarah said, putting a comforting hand on his shoulder. "This was just a bad night." She looked behind her and surveyed the scene. "We all could have been hurt, including the horses. Instead, we lost a few tents and saddles. And

it's awful that a few acres of woods were burned. But we're all safe—because of *you*."

It was true. Will had remained calm throughout the whole ordeal and had led everyone to safety.

Will finally managed to look up at Sarah. Then he looked over at Alma, Molly, Chloe, Zoey, and all the horses. He gave a small smile and then said, "I sure hope my aunt and uncle see it that way."

Nearby, the horses were grazing.

Calypso looked over at Jimber. "Your human sure came through when things got a little scary back there," she told him.

Jimber felt proud. "He's not bad—as far as humans go."

"Sometimes I wish they'd have a little more common horse sense," said Scarlet.

Button agreed. "Yeah, a little of that would have gone a long way tonight," she said.

"It was just an accident," Calypso reminded the group.

"Humans make mistakes," Jimber said somberly, as he looked across at the destructive fire. Then he looked back at Will and the other kids. "But they can sure be brave helping each other when they're needed."

None of the horses could argue with that.

# CHAPTER 11

**A**cross the lake, the firefighters had finally gotten the blaze under control. Bailey had notified them of the fire, and because he knew where the campsite was, he helped lead the firefighters to the exact location. Then he went in search of Will and the girls. When he finally found them on other side of the lake, he was relieved.

"The whole time, I didn't know if you all

were hurt, or worse!" Bailey told them. "I must have hit redial a hundred times!"

Will took out the cell phone from his pocket. It was dripping with water. He chuckled. "Guess this phone doesn't work underwater," he said, and everyone laughed.

The laughter from the kids caused the horses to look over and see what was going on.

Button turned back to the others and said, "Do the *horses* get the credit for saving the humans?" She shook her head. "Probably not."

"There better be some fresh oats and some serious grooming time waiting for us when we get home!" added Scarlet.

The horses knew they were the real heroes of the day. They wished the humans recognized that. But the horses were in for a little surprise. . . .

Sarah walked up to the horses. "Let's get you guys home now," she said, and got up on Scarlet. "We couldn't have done it without you!"

"Yeah!" agreed Molly, giving her horse a hug. "Way to go, Calypso!"

"*Muy bueno*, Button!" Alma said. "Very good!"

The horses whinnied happily—they *were* appreciated after all!

Finally, just before sunrise, the group began the long trek home.

"Race you back!" Molly proposed.

"Maybe we better not," replied Alma. "We'd probably slide off!"

Behind them, Chloe and Zoey were arguing.

"I told you a few drops of water wasn't enough to douse the fire," Chloe said.

"You did not!" said Zoey.

"Did so!" insisted Chloe.

Even though they were sisters, they had no problem blaming each other.

"Zoey, what does Mom always tell you about being more responsible?" asked Chloe.

"Me?!" exclaimed Zoey. "*You're* the one who always gets us in trouble, Chloe! You're the big sister. You're older. You're supposed to know everything. That's what you're always telling me!"

Zoey and Chloe gave each other dirty looks and rode on in silence.

Meanwhile, Bailey and Will rode next to each other at the back of the procession.

Will took a deep breath and looked over at his cousin. "Bailey, I don't know what your folks are thinking, but there's no excuse for—"

"They'll understand, Will," Bailey interrupted. "They know mistakes happen."

Will looked hopeful. That wasn't what he was expecting to hear.

"Trust me," Bailey continued. "My parents will definitely understand. Besides, Chloe and Zoey's parents will be getting the big bill from the forest service for putting out the fire. Not to mention the bill from Horseland for the lost gear."

Will felt a sense of relief. He grinned and said, "Good thing they can afford it!"

Shep, Angora, and Teeny continue their walk along the edge of the lake and look out over the charred landscape. They again see evidence of the previous night's raging fire. The destruction is shocking, and the pungent smell of smoke still lingers in the air.

"I thought it was bad when we tipped over a flowerpot or tracked mud into the humans' house," Teeny says, not believing what she sees. "But this place is awful!"

"Humans can be great," says Shep. "But when they get careless, they can seriously mess things up."

"When *we* make a mess, humans yell at us and shoo us away," Teeny points out.

Angora looks over at Teeny. "What else can they do? It's not as if we can fix it."

Shep agrees. "It's easier for them. They have hands. They can use tools. And sometimes that means they have to try to fix what they've broken."

Just then, the trio sees Chloe and Zoey up ahead. The two girls are on their knees, using trowels to plant saplings in the burned ground. The animals watch from a distance.

Covered in dirt, Chloe feels exhausted and fed up. "How many of these trees do we have to plant?" she complains. There seem to be so many to plant—and there are. The fire burned down a lot of trees.

At that moment, a forest ranger appears. Furious about the forest destruction, he has no interest in and isn't going to stand for Chloe's complaints.

"Uh . . . I guess we have to keep going until we replace all the ones we burned," Zoey says quickly. She smiles halfheartedly at the ranger.

Chloe sighs and picks up her trowel again. "We'll be here *forever*! All of this because we thought hauling up the water was just too much work."

Of course, both Chloe and Zoey now realize how silly and careless that decision was and certainly not worth the risk they took.

But Chloe still wants to get out of planting all the trees. "What if we just—" she began.

Luckily, Zoey is there to keep her on track. "Oh, no! Not again! You just keeping digging, sister!"

And that's just what they did.

# Meet the Riders and Their Horses

**Sarah Whitney** is a natural when it comes to horses. Sarah's horse, **Scarlet**, is a black Arabian mare.

**Alma Rodriquez** is confident and hard-working. Alma's horse, **Button**, is a skewbald pinto mare.

**Molly Washington** has a great sense of humor and doesn't take anything seriously—except her riding. Molly's horse, **Calypso**, is a spotted Appaloosa mare.

**Chloe Stilton** is often forceful and very competitive, even when it comes to her sister, Zoey. Chloe's horse, **Chili**, is a gray Dutch Warmblood stallion.

**Zoey Stilton**
is Chloe's sister. She's also very competitive and spoiled. Zoey's horse, **Pepper**, is a gray Dutch Warmblood mare.

**Bailey Handler**
likes to take chances. His parents own Horseland Ranch. Bailey's horse, **Aztec**, is a Kiger mustang.

86

**Will Taggert** is Bailey's cousin and has lived with the family since he was little. Because he's the oldest, Will is in charge when the adults aren't around. Will's horse, **Jimber**, is a palomino stallion.

# *Spotlight on Jimber*

Breed: Palomino★

★**Hold your horses!**
Different breeds of horses can be palominos!
In reality, palomino is a horse *color*, not a breed.
Palomino horses are usually Quarter horses, Arabians,
Morgans, Tennessee Walking horses,
and American Saddlebreds.

## Physical Characteristic:
🐎 Golden coloring

## Personality:
🐎 Strong

🐎 Loyal

🐎 Good temperament

## Fun facts:
🐎 Queen Isabella of Spain loved palominos.
In 1519, Cortés brought some of the
queen's palominos with him to America.

88

🐴 Due to their lovely golden color, palominos stand out in a show ring. They are often used as parade horses, too.

🐴 The TV horse Mr. Ed was a palomino.

# ♡ Will's ♡
# Bareback Riding Tips

With the proper guidance, riding a horse without a saddle is a great way to learn how to keep your balance. Here are some helpful hints to make your bareback ride a safe one.

### Before you ride:

- ♞ Before riding bareback, you should be able to ride in a saddle without relying on the use of stirrups.
- ♞ When learning, make sure an experienced

rider or instructor is there with you to assist or watch.

🐎 Wear a helmet.

🐎 Ride a tame horse that you're familiar with.

## Mounting:

🐎 Because you don't have stirrups to help you mount the horse, have a friend help you up or use a mounting block.

🐎 Holding onto the reins, place your hands on the horse's neck and throw your leg over the horse's back. If you don't have reins, you can hold on to the horse's mane.

## While riding:

🐎 Make sure to sit closer to the withers than to the horse's back.

🐎 Don't lean forward. Keep your back straight and your eyes forward.

🐎 To make the horse walk, simply use pressure from your legs, especially below the knees.

🐎 Keep your heels down. This will help you use only your lower legs, and keep you relaxed from the knees up.

♘ Hold on.

♘ Remember to relax and enjoy the ride!

## Dismounting:

♘ To dismount, bring your leg back over the horse's back and slide off.